THIS BOOK BELONGS TO:

_____

OTHER MY FRIEND PARIS BOOKS

My Twins are Coming Home

My Twins' First Birthday

My Twins' First Halloween

My Twins' First Christmas

Published by:

New Year Publishing, LLC   144 Diablo Ranch Ct.   Danville, CA 94506 USA

orders@newyearpublishing.com   http://www.newyearpublishing.com

© 2008 by New Year Publishing, LLC All rights reserved.

Library of Congress Control Number: 2007930313

ISBN: 978-0976009542

NEW YEAR
PUBLISHING, LLC.

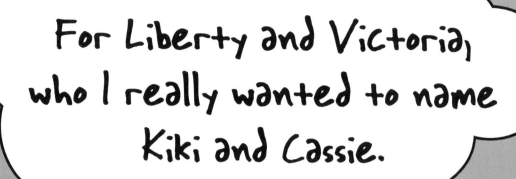

My name is Paris.
I am three years
old and I live near
San Francisco,
California with my
Mommy and Daddy.

Some mornings I go to preschool.
Other days Mommy and I play with our friends.
On rainy days Mommy and I usually bake.

I'm going to be A Big Sister.
My Mommy has two babies inside her tummy.

Today is the 4th of July. At night the three of us watched the fireworks and I curled up on Mommy's lap.

Sometimes I have sleepovers at Grandma and Papa's house. They have a big garden, which I like.

I'm not so sure about all of this. Will I have to share my room with them? My toys?

Daddy and I go fun places on the weekends so Mommy can rest. We went to the zoo today. I liked the giraffes the best.

Apparently this two baby thing is called twins. I have been thinking about names for MY twins. Cinderella? Elmo?

Two of my Mommy's friends threw us a party called a Baby Shower. I got books about being A Big Sister and twin dollies. There was a really yummy cake there.

It's Halloween, my favorite holiday! Daddy helped me into my dragon costume and took me trick or treating. I got lots of candy.

Bedrest. That's what it's called when
Mommy stays in bed all day. Our friends come
over every day and bring us lunch. She and I do
lots of puzzles and read together in her bed.

I sometimes feel MY twins move inside my Mommy's tummy. What are they doing in there all squished together?

Today Daddy and I test drove all different kinds of cars. Mommy wants an SUV but Daddy and I aren't so sure that we do.

We don't go out as much as we used to. We do
Family Movie Night a lot now, with popcorn.

I got a Big Girl Bed today and new sheets!
My room is lavender, my favorite color.
I think I'm going to like being A Big Sister.

The big day is here! I got dropped off at Grandma and Papa's house on the way to the hospital and soon we'll meet MY twins. I'm going to be THE BEST BIG SISTER EVER!

CPSIA information can be obtained
at www.ICGtesting.com
Printed in the USA
LVIC082119210213
321243LV00002B